Emoji Adventures #2

Emoji Olympics

ISBN 978-0692655047

#BoredGames

Dot, Billy, and I are in my living room playing Monopoly with Billy's older brother, Todd. Todd is, unlike Billy, an amazing athlete. Any athlete knows that competitive games require perfect concentration, but right now Todd can't focus. There's a good reason why: he's waiting to hear if he's been selected to the pole vault team for the upcoming Olympics.

"Do not pass 'Go'. Do not collect two hundred dollars," Billy reads from the Chance card he just pulled. "Aw, man! That's the third time I've gotten that card this game."

To add insult to injury, he's suddenly hit in the face with a stream of water. Even Todd jumps in surprise. My devilish brother Kevin stands in the doorway with a giant squirt soaker. Behind him is his robot SAM - short for Sister Annoying Machine. So today SAM is doing exactly what he's programed to do - bother me.

"Why do you always have to be so..." I begin.

"—hilarious!" Dot interrupts.

"I was going to say *annoying*," I say.

As if to illustrate my point, SAM shoots me with a giant stream of water.

If I weren't so used to this behavior, I wouldn't have known to duck just in time.

"Stop it!" I cry.

"Stop it!" SAM repeats.

"Stop recording us!" I yell to Kevin.

"Did you plan this as a distraction so you could rig the cards?" Billy asks his brother.

"Yeah, right," Todd says. "As if I'm worried about Monopoly right now."

"It's all an act," Billy jokes, in a deadpan voice making him sound completely serious. "We all know Todd is a huge cheater."

Dot – who sometimes misses the joke because she's too distracted by the boys in the room – punches Billy's arm. "That's not true!" she says. "Todd is great at everything he tries!"

For this compliment, she receives a blast of water from my brother in the back of the head. While she giggles, I chase him out of the room.

 "Let's get back to the game," I say.

"So where were we?" Todd asks.

It's clear he hasn't been paying attention at all.

I'm nervous for Todd, but smile through it, which is easy considering my smile is frozen across my face almost all the time.

"You'll get picked for the team," I say enthusiastically. "We believe in you."

"Do you really think so?" Todd asks.

"I do," says a voice from the door. It's Billy and Todd's mother, Mrs. Brown, who's bursting with excitement and grinning ear to ear. My parents flank her, also eager to hear the news.

"We just heard! Todd's been selected for the Olympic pole vaulting team!"

#MeetThePress

 By the next morning, everyone in Emojiville knows Todd's exciting news. Reporters and paparazzi are everywhere, waiting for Todd to emerge from his house, which happens to be across the street from mine. Dot is outside waiting for Billy and me so we can ride our bikes to school.

"The whole town is in a frenzy," a newscaster says into his microphone. "And rumor has it, there's going to be an official parade honoring Todd this weekend."

"A parade?!" Dot's eyes light up even more .

Todd appears, looking happy and also a little overwhelmed. A sea of reporters swarm him as cameras flash non-stop.

The reporters pepper Todd with questions:

"Were you surprised by the news?"

"What's your training schedule?"

"Do you plan on winning?"

"Of course." Todd answers the last question with a confident smile.

Behind him, a dapper figure in a tuxedo and top hat emerges. A few seconds pass before Dot and I recognize who it is.

"Billy?!" Dot asks.

Billy waves and tips his hat as a dozen cameras snap pictures. He makes sure the cameras are still on him then blows kisses and waves, even offering to autograph a reporter's notepad.

OMG.

Finally Billy joins us and we bike 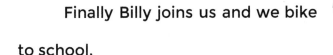 to school.

"I'm so excited for your brother," Dot says.

Billy nods proudly. "It's a huge victory for us."

For *us?* I think. What did *you* do?

A reporter on a bike catches up to us, with one hand on the handlebars and the other holding a recorder.

"Hey, Billy!" the reporter calls out. "Chuck Jones, Emoji Daily News. Are you willing to answer a few questions?"

"Absolutely!" Billy grins.

"We don't have time!" I protest. "We're going to be late for school."

But when we get to the parking lot, there are even more reporters waiting. As soon as they see Billy, they run toward him, snapping pictures and yelling out questions.

"Billy, you're famous!" Dot whispers.

"I know!" Billy whispers, bouncing excitedly on his heels.

I'm about to disagree with him –
Todd is the famous one; Billy's just his kid brother. But I'm interrupted by reporters calling his name:

"Billy! Billy!"

It looks like Billy really *is* famous now.

#TrainingSession

 Once school is out, we head to Emojiville Stadium, home to this year's Summer Olympics. Emojiville Stadium is the biggest arena in town (actually, it's the *only* arena in town.) But today it feels bigger than ever with all the excitement. Todd is outside the stadium doing sprints, practicing harder

than he's ever worked before. The three

of us encourage him and try to keep up.

"You've got this!" Billy shouts.

"Great form, Todd!" Dot calls out.

Billy and I shake our heads, embarrassed.

Across the street from the stadium, a rehearsal for the opening ceremony is taking place. It's going to be a huge spectacle, with elaborate displays and participants from all over the world. There are dancers, acrobats, and musicians from hundreds of countries, all here in our local stadium.

There are also dozens of colorful flags waving in the breeze. Some flags I recognize, like France, Brazil, Japan, Mexico, and Canada. Other flags, I've never seen before. I see Mrs. Zimmerman in the stands and hope she's not getting any ideas about quizzing us on these flags after the games.

Todd joins the Emojiville team and waves the flag in front of a group of kindergartners who watch and cheer from the stands.

"GO, TODD, GO!" they chant.

Billy, who's still wearing his tuxedo and top hat, walks around shaking people's hands, passing out business cards to the adults and lollipops to the kids.

"You could say talent runs in the family," he says proudly. "Be sure to follow me on Snapchat."

"Did Billy just kiss that baby?" Dot asks.

Billy stops to take a selfie with a group of screaming teenage girls.

"Be sure to tag me," he says, then makes a peace sign. "#CoolBillyBrown!"

He kisses the hand of another girl who faints.

I groan. Why is Billy acting like this is *his* big day? I feel annoyed, but also know people expect me to be positive. So I tune him out and focus on what's happening on the field.

The whole town is so proud of Todd – he's the first resident of Emojiville to make the Olympics team in over fifty years, so it's perfect they're taking place

right here in town.

It's a pretty good day to

be living in Emojiville.

#TheInterview

Later Billy, Dot, and I go back to my house to work on our science project. Instead, we end up watching the Olympic coverage on my phone. The newscaster interviews competitors from several countries in every sport. They also introduce this year's Olympic mascot – an adorable panda named Panji who dances up and down the aisles of the stadium.

"I hope they interview a soccer player next." The only thing Dot loves more than boys is soccer.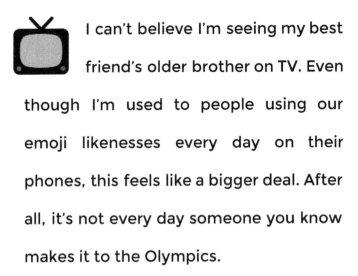

But instead of a soccer player, Todd suddenly appears on the screen, fresh from another run.

"OMG!!!" we all cheer.

I can't believe I'm seeing my best friend's older brother on TV. Even though I'm used to people using our emoji likenesses every day on their phones, this feels like a bigger deal. After all, it's not every day someone you know makes it to the Olympics.

Todd answers questions about his love of pole vaulting, his lifelong dream of being in the Olympics, and what life is like here in Emojiville. At one point, he mentions his family.

"He's talking about me!" Billy exclaims.

We all gasp when a picture of Billy fills the screen.

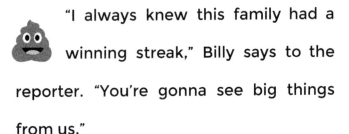 "I always knew this family had a winning streak," Billy says to the reporter. "You're gonna see big things from us."

Once they cut away to another athlete, Billy turns to Dot and me. "Aren't you guys excited to be best friends with a celebrity?"

For one of the few times in my life, I frown. "You know this doesn't have anything to do with you, right? It's your brother's accomplishment, not yours."

"Somebody sounds jealous," Billy says.

I know I'm supposed to be positive, but Billy is starting to get on my nerves. I get being proud of his brother, but he's taking this a bit too far.

After Dot and Billy have gone home, Kevin pops his head into my room. "Hey Annie! Why's your horse book in the fireplace?"

"Yeah, right." He's tricked me too many times for me to believe him now. I check my pocket to make sure he hasn't hidden my phone again.

"I have something cool to show you," he says.

I ignore him.

"Wow, I've never seen you so crabby."

"I'm just annoyed." The words spill out. "Billy keeps showing off just because Todd's in the Olympics. It's driving me crazy! I almost can't wait for all this to be over."

Kevin nods sympathetically. "You just think he should take it down a notch, right?"

"Exactly." Who knew Kevin could be so easy to talk to?

"That can be arranged," Kevin says.

"Wait, what?"

Kevin's grin gets even wider. "Leave everything to me."

"We're just talking," I say. "I'm not saying we should *do* anything."

"I got this," Kevin says.

"You've got what?"

But he's gone.

When I go to bed that night, I have an uneasy feeling in the pit of my stomach. Did I just make a deal with the devil?

#Scandal

 The school is abuzz with nonstop chatter about how great Todd is and, surprisingly, Billy too.

That all changes at lunch. Suddenly people are confused and glued to their phones.

"Did you hear the news?" Dot asks.

"They're saying Todd's a cheater!"

I go to the news app and see a clip posted by the local TV station. *BREAKING NEWS: TODD BROWN IS A CHEATER,* says the headline.

I've never seen Dot look so glum.

"And all this time I thought he was Prince Charming," she sighs.

Todd, a cheater? I've known him practically my entire life and have never once caught him cheating.

"I don't understand." I turn to Dot. "Why does everyone think he cheats?"

My question is answered before we leave the table. The news station announces they have footage of Todd's own brother – Billy Brown – saying Todd's a cheater.

Dot and I watch the footage together in horror.

"We all know Todd is a huge cheater," Billy says to a room full of people.

"Wait a minute," I say. "Is that my living room?"

"We're in the video," Dot says.

It hits me like a ton of bricks. Kevin used the footage from SAM's robot cam when they crashed our Monopoly game last week. When I complained about Billy last night, I didn't mean for Kevin to pull that recording out. Billy was only kidding!

By the end of the day, the video is all over social media. Someone even made a dance video on YouTube using the audio clip in a song. (It already has half a million views.)

For the rest of the day, all anyone wants to talk about is the scandal with Todd. People post memes that show embarrassing pictures of Todd with the caption CHEATER. I can't imagine how Todd must feel with everyone hurling such an ugly accusation.

I look everywhere for Billy, desperate to explain what happened. It's hard to keep smiling, knowing that I've done something to hurt one of my friends.

When I finally find Billy in the parking lot surrounded by paparazzi, he's already figured out what happened.

"How could you do this to my brother?" he asks furiously.

Before I can respond, he turns and runs away, chased by reporters.

WHERE IS MY DEVIL BROTHER?! I look all over the school before finding him in the library with his friends reading skateboard magazines. I bet he's trying to hide from me – that's the only reason Kevin would be in the library.

"Why did you do that?" I ask. "Billy is furious!"

"He was getting on your nerves," Kevin answers.

"He's my friend and you've ruined his life," I say. "I thought we were going to poke fun at Billy, not use his own words against Todd!"

But my devil-of-a-brother only smiles. "You should've known who you were dealing with," he says, "when you spilled your guts."

"You're the worst brother ever!" I shout.

The librarian shushes me and hurries me out of the room.

#HowCouldYou

 By evening, everyone in town has heard that Todd is a cheater, including my parents. The whole family watches the news for updates on the story.

I can hardly look Kevin in the eyes. I'm not used to being mad. I actually like being happy, but I have every reason to be upset. Kevin has gone too far.

"This just in," the anchorwoman reports. "The Olympic Committee has announced that in order to get to the bottom of this scandal, Todd will be given a tinkle test."

A tinkle test for a poop head?

The anchorman next to her nods sadly. "This is a huge disappointment for the whole town. I hope Todd and his family know this is a stain on their name."

"Yeah, a poop stain!" Kevin laughs.

I sink in my seat knowing I'm partially responsible for the shaming of my best friend's family. Why was I so mad at Billy anyhow? Sure, he was being annoying, but by wanting to teach him a lesson, *I* became the annoying one. No, not just annoying. Mean.

"This is terrible," Mom says.

"It's all Kevin's fault!" I say.

"You blame Kevin for everything," Mom says.

"Because he's a devil!"

"Annie, I will not stand for that kind of talk about your brother," Mom says.

Suddenly there's a knock at the door, so forceful I know right away who it is: Billy and Todd, both madder than I've ever seen them.

"How could you?!" Todd asks.

"I never accused Todd of cheating," Billy says. "I don't care what your robot heard."

I look at Kevin, expecting him to gloat, but for once he isn't smiling. Maybe he understands he was a little too devilish this time around.

Billy looks me in the eye.

"You need to fix this," he says.

"I will," I promise.

But how?

#Brainstorm

 Dot comes over later to help Kevin and me brainstorm ways to solve this giant problem.

I'm mad at Kevin, but I know in order to restore Todd's honor I'll need Kevin's skills. So I return to my usual cheerful self and for the first time in his life, it looks like Kevin actually wants to help.

The three of us sit in the backyard.

Freckles, our cat, rests peacefully in Dot's

lap.

 "What we need to do is prove

Todd is a great guy," Kevin says.

"I've got it!" Dot shouts. "We could

have a photo shoot."

"How would that help?" I ask.

Dot thinks about it. "It would show that Todd was... handsome?"

Kevin rolls his eyes.

"What if we interview his coach?" I suggest. "We all know Todd's a great team player. His coach can vouch for him!"

"They interviewed the coach yesterday," Kevin says. "He was so upset, it wasn't helpful at all."

Freckles jumps out of Dot's lap, startling everybody. She hisses at Kevin before settling in with me.

"I've got it!" Kevin exclaims.

"The three of us can collect all the stray cats in Emojiville. Then we'll set up a cat adoption center in front of the pet store with a big banner with Todd's name. We'll find homes for all the stray cats in town. No one will think Todd's a bad guy after that."

It's not the best plan, but at least it's a start. Maybe Kevin has a few good ideas after all.

#Meow

 The three of us spend the week searching for stray cats. At first we look as a group, but then realize we'll work more quickly if we split up. Dot and I paint a giant banner that reads *TODD BROWN CARES ABOUT CATS.*

Usually there are lots of strays that hang around the playground, and I figure some of them might need homes.

When I get to the front of the schoolyard, I immediately see a cat. I'm worried she might run away, but instead she leaps into my arms. Perfect! Sometimes a big smile is all it takes to win over a cuddly creature. She's a sweet, gray cat with a friendly face, just like mine.

I go off to look for others but have no luck. Will Dot and Kevin be mad if I show up with only one cat?

On my way, I see Dot on her own with no cats in sight.

"You couldn't even find *one*?" I ask.

"I found one, but then I passed by a soccer game and started watching. By the time it was over, the cat was gone," Dot explains.

You can never rely on Dot for anything except loving soccer.

I walk quickly to the pet store, worried that Kevin won't have found any cats either. It won't look good if Todd's adoption center only has one cat. Maybe we can tell everyone the day was a huge success and all the other cats found homes.

As soon as I get to the pet store, I realize how wrong I was. Kevin has found close to twenty cats!

"Where did you find all these cats?!" I ask.

He shrugs. "Around."

A news crew is already here reporting on Todd's amazing cat rescue and a crowd of people *ooh* and *ahh* at all the adorable animals. I place my cat with the others. They all seem to get along well.

"It looks like Todd Brown does have some good qualities," a reporter says, stroking a tabby.

I'm relieved to see that everything is going according to plan. I can't wait to tell Billy who's responsible for saving the Brown family name.

But a new group of people appear at the store and they do not look happy.

"I just saw my cat on TV," yells a woman in curlers and house slippers. "They said she was up for adoption!"

As if on cue, a cat leaps into her arms.

"Don't worry, Lucy," the woman tells the cat. "You're safe now."

"Some kid swiped Spike right off my front porch!" an angry man shouts.

More people show up looking for their cats. Everyone is incredibly mad.

Did Kevin steal twenty cats? That's a new low, even for him.

It turns out the cat I found was a stray that wants to stay that way. She runs off before I can find her a home.

After seeing the charity on the news, Todd and Billy show up too. They think the town will be thrilled, but instead they're even worse off than before.

"We return with breaking news," the newscaster reports. "It appears Todd

Brown is not only a cheater but a cat-napper too."

"Cat-napper?" Billy asks.

Todd appears at his side. "C'mon, let's get out of here before we're chased out."

How could I have been so stupid to trust Kevin again?

I look everywhere to find him, but in classic Kevin fashion, he's already gone.

Dot and I return all the cats to their rightful owners.

I finally head home, looking for my mischief-making brother. He and I have some unfinished business to discuss.

#OffTheList

 I'm not used to being this upset because I know things tend to work out if you have a positive attitude. I decide to take five minutes to breathe so I can think more clearly.

My plan is foiled when I walk into the house and see Kevin hanging out in the living room with SAM.

"You didn't tell me the cats were stolen!" I say.

"You liked the idea," Kevin says.

"Of *stray* cats, not stolen!" I reply.

"I was just trying to help." Kevin says.

I don't believe him. "Well, stop trying to help because you only make things worse."

SAM has been silently reaching for my pocket and is getting ready to steal my phone - *again*.

"Knock it off!" I say.

I'm about to get my parents when there's another knock on

the door. It's Billy and he looks even more upset than last time.

"You're ruining everything for my whole family," Billy says in tears. "I thought you were my friend."

I feel so guilty that I don't know how to respond. "I *am* your friend," I finally say.

"If you were my friend, you wouldn't try to sabotage Todd."

"I can explain," I start.

But Billy turns away in disgust, leaving me standing by the front door.

 It's so heart-wrenching that even Kevin seems to feel guilty.

"I'm going to find Todd and talk to him," I say.

When Kevin offers to join me, I'm too sad to protest. I don't know how to handle all these negative feelings, especially knowing this whole fiasco is partially my fault.

 We run into Dot on our way to Emojiville Stadium.

"At least everyone got their cats back." Like me, Dot tries to look on the bright side.

There's a guard in front of the stadium with a list of visitors who are allowed to enter. Yesterday we had no trouble getting into the stadium to watch Todd practice. But when we give our names to the guard today, he shakes his head.

"You've been removed from the list," he says. "I don't know why you'd even want to be associated with a cheater like Todd Brown anyway."

I look at Dot in disbelief.

"I heard he stole twenty cats and tried selling them online," the guard continues. "Can you believe it?"

I explain that's not what happened but he doesn't seem to care.

"Does this mean I won't get to see the Olympic soccer team practice?" Dot asks sadly.

"Even worse," I say. "It means we're back to square one. We have to clear Todd's name without him knowing we're doing it."

#ANewPlan

I finally get to talk to Billy at school the next day. Yesterday he was so upset he wouldn't let me explain what happened, but at least here at school there's nowhere for him to go.

"You have to understand," I begin. "The video fiasco and the botched cat rescue both happened because my brother is the *devil*. I won't be foolish enough to trust him anymore. I still really want to clear Todd's name but won't be asking Kevin for help again. Instead, I want *you* to help. You're the closest person in the world to Todd. You'll know how to fix this."

Billy is still angry, but he can tell I feel horrible. He also knows this might be the only way to clear Todd's name.

"Okay," he finally says. "But you have to promise Kevin won't try to help this time."

"Believe me, I promise." I'm never going to even *talk* to Kevin again.

We start working on another plan.

"Even though Kevin's idea was a disaster, I think he was right about making Todd look like a hero," I say. "That seems like the surest way to get some good press."

Dot and Billy agree.

"We could have a photo shoot," Dot suggests.

"That was your idea last time!" I say.

Dot blushes. "Whoops."

"We could bring him to school to teach everyone how to pole vault," I suggest.

Billy shakes his head. "No one wants to learn from someone they think is a cheater. And besides, Todd's too busy training. He needs to spend all day at the stadium practicing for the competition, assuming he's not disqualified."

Disqualified?! We have to act fast!

A few feet away, I notice a girl trying to open her locker with a broken arm. Her friends have all drawn on her cast with colorful markers.

"I know," I say. "The three of us can volunteer at the Children's Hospital! We'll tell them we're with the *Todd Brown Helps Children* fund. If they say they've never heard of it, we'll say that's because Todd doesn't like to brag about his charity work."

"I love it!" Dot says.

Of course she does. However, Billy doesn't seem too convinced. But we don't have a lot of time or ideas.

"Fine," he finally agrees.

Children's Hospital it is.

#Volunteering

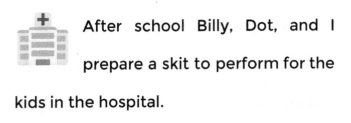 After school Billy, Dot, and I prepare a skit to perform for the kids in the hospital.

We spend the next day gathering costumes and props. We get a big sheet, a pair of plastic fangs, a witch's hat, and a cauldron. It's everything we need to entertain the kids – and save Todd's reputation.

We arrive at the Children's Hospital, and quickly put on our costumes. I put on the witch's hat, Dot wears the fangs, and Billy covers himself in the sheet.

"You must be here with the *Todd Brown Helps Children* fund," the nurse says.

"That's right," Dot mumbles through her fangs.

I give the nurse my famous smile. "We can't wait to perform for the kids."

She leads us to a big room where a group of children are waiting and as soon as we walk in, they cheer. It feels great to be doing something so positive. For the first time in days, I feel like my happy self.

"Hi, everyone," I say. "Welcome to Monster High."

We perform our skit about a trio of friends just like us who happen to be monsters instead of emojis. Dot plays a lovestruck vampire, Billy an unlucky ghost, and I'm an upbeat witch.

We pull out all the stops - singing, dancing, and trying to be scary. Even though the three of us aren't performers, we know how high the stakes are and give it our all. The kids love it.

"I've never performed like this in my life," Dot whispers. "I'm glad it's for a good cause."

"*Two* good causes," Billy corrects. "For the children *and* my brother."

Afterward, we go around the wing and visit kids in their rooms to cheer them up. But a doctor marches in wearing a surgical mask. One of his eyes is as red as a stop sign.

"Stop the act! Stop the act!" the doctor barks.

"What's the matter?" I ask.

"And what's wrong with your eye?" Dot asks.

"I just got pink eye," the doctor says. "And the nurse who let you in has it too!"

Billy takes off the sheet. "Why is everyone getting pink eye?" he asks.

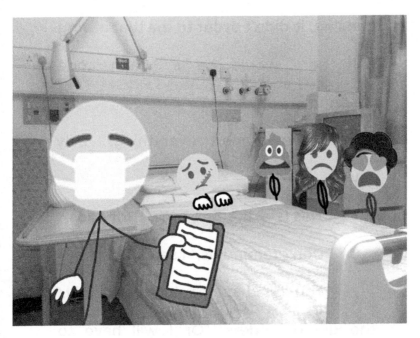

As soon as the doctor sees Billy, he gasps. "Probably because of you! Who let fecal material into a hospital to entertain sick children? Bacteria - hello? 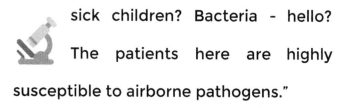 The patients here are highly susceptible to airborne pathogens."

In the middle of all that singing and dancing, it didn't occur to me that having Billy here would be a health code violation.

"We've ruined everything!" Billy says.

"This isn't the first time," Dot adds.

"Don't remind us," I say.

"You need to leave immediately," the doctor orders. "Or I will have to quarantine all of you."

We don't need to be told twice.

We leave the hospital and put our heads together (not literally, because now we're all worried about getting pink eye.) It seems everything we do gets us deeper and deeper into trouble.

How do we clear Todd's name?

#MyWorstNightmare

We bike to the playground, hoping to blow off some steam on the swings. However when we get there, the mood is so low, we're sure something has happened. Dot checks her phone and it's clear from her face the news isn't good.

"What's up?" Billy asks.

"You tell him." Dot shows me her phone.

BREAKING NEWS: TODD BROWN BANNED FROM OLYMPICS reads the top story on the Emojiville Times. My heart sinks.

I expect Billy to start screaming but instead he's silent, which is even worse.

"This was bound to happen." He collapses on the swings.

The past week has been upsetting for all of us but this is the worst possible news.

"Billy, I'm so sorry," I say from the bottom of my heart. "I never would've encouraged Kevin to prank you if I'd known it would get Todd disqualified. I should have just talked to you instead of trying to teach you a lesson."

"It's okay," Billy says. "We all make mistakes."

Billy might be the nicest person I've ever met.

"It's going to be humiliating carrying the torch at the opening ceremony tomorrow," he says.

I totally forgot about tomorrow's opening ceremony! After Todd got chosen for the Olympic team, our whole school was invited to participate in the giant gala. Even though Todd was just banned, our school isn't. We're expected to march proudly across the field. Too bad I don't feel very proud right now.

As I go to sleep that night, I wonder if there's still a way for Todd to save face. I lie in bed racking my brain for ideas. Nothing comes. The Olympic Games could've been great, could've been a real accomplishment. But now I don't even want to go.

#OpeningCeremonies

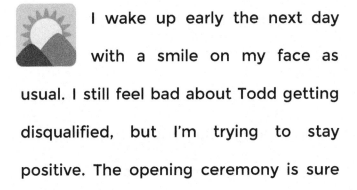I wake up early the next day with a smile on my face as usual. I still feel bad about Todd getting disqualified, but I'm trying to stay positive. The opening ceremony is sure to be an incredible event.

It seems like forever before we can finally leave. I walk over to the stadium with my family; none of us can believe the big day is actually here.

"I'm so excited," Mom gushes.

"I am too," Dad says. "Although I wish they'd accepted my brilliant new torch invention for the opening ceremony."

"Your 'invention' was just three flashlights taped together," I remind him.

"Yeah, but customized with flags of every country," Dad adds. "The souvenirs alone would have made a fortune."

When we get to the stadium, I can't believe how beautiful it is. It's been a spectacle all week, but today there's a giant Ferris wheel in the middle of the arena and colorful lights on every row.

There are more people here than I've ever seen in one place before. Even though everyone in town is upset that we no longer have a representative in the games, we're still thrilled to be at the Olympics.

Along the sidelines, all of my classmates are waiting, except for one. I can't find Billy anywhere.

I ask Tiffany and Zoe if they've seen him. They shake their heads no.

"He's probably hiding somewhere, hoping everyone forgets his brother's a cheater," Tiffany says.

"I'd never show my face again if I were him," Zoe chimes in.

I leave the haters before they say anything else. I find Dot and ask her if she's seen Billy.

"I don't know if he's going to show today," Dot says. "Todd isn't even allowed to walk with us while we carry the torch. He has to sit in the stands."

"Maybe that's where Billy is." But to my relief he suddenly appears beside me.

"You're here!"

"I just wish Todd were walking next to me," Billy says sadly.

I try to console him but loud horns blare. The ceremony is about to begin! I can't help but feel another rush of excitement. We line up in rows, ready to enter the stadium on cue.

From the sidelines, we watch as an elderly woman lights the torch. The audience bursts into thunderous applause as the old woman looks up with a smile almost as big as mine.

 "She was the most famous tennis player in the world in the 1940s," Dot explains.

"How'd you know that?" I'm surprised Dot is knowledgeable about any sport other than soccer.

"I've been studying up on the games," Dot says with a proud smile.

"Who knows? Maybe someday *I'll* end up in the Olympics."

Principal Lopez gives us the signal when it's our school's turn to march. The whole school enters the arena, in the middle of all the action. Fireworks go off overhead and confetti and streamers fly everywhere. In the crowd, people wave flags from every country. It feels like the whole world is here in Emojiville for this celebration.

From the field, I can see Todd sitting with his family. Not sitting – slumping. He looks miserable to be here. I would be miserable too if everyone thought I was a cheater and banned me from doing the sport I love. Seeing Todd at his lowest in the middle of Emojiville's brightest moment, I feel a little less festive.

"Todd!" I call out, waving.

Todd sees me but doesn't wave back. He's clearly still angry. Still, I try to stay positive and continue walking with my classmates.

Everyone applauds when the Ferris wheel starts turning. This must be the grand finale, because there are even more fireworks and streamers than before.

One of the passengers on the Ferris wheel is Panji, the funny panda mascot I saw at practice the other day. His crazy dance will surely end up on YouTube. Everyone in the audience laughs and cheers him on. Even Billy, who's had trouble smiling all day, can't help but chuckle at the panda's moves.

But without warning, the Ferris wheel grinds to a halt when the panda's car reaches the top. The panda stops dancing and looks around for instructions.

The person in the panda suit screams, waving his arms wildly.

Everyone looks around, trying to decide what to do. Some run to find help; some shoot videos on their phones, while others are frozen in horror.

"What can we do?" Dot asks.

"I have no idea." But then I do. And
it might be just the idea that sets
everything right with Todd.

#SaveThePanda

I dart through my classmates, still staring at the stranded panda hovering in the evening sky.

"Where are you going?" Dot calls.

I don't have time to answer. I run through the crowd toward the bleachers, until I reach the person I'm trying to find: Todd.

"You're the only person who can save the mascot!"

"Me?!" Todd asks. "How can *I* help?"

"Think about it," I say.

His face lights up. "I can pole vault up to get to him!"

"Exactly!"

"But wait," Todd says. "I'm banned from the field."

"You're an Olympic athlete," I say. "There's no way they'll be able to catch you."

He smiles, knowing I'm right.

"Go show everyone you're a good guy," I say. "Because you *are.*"

Todd thinks about what I'm saying.
(Sometimes a little positivity goes a long
way.) He rises from his seat and charges
toward the field. People whip their heads
around as he passes by, faster than
lightning.

 "Wait!" a man shouts. "Don't let
that cheater on the field!"

But no one is any match for
Todd's agility. He leaps over the partition
between the crowd and the field,
dashing full speed toward the Ferris
wheel.

Suddenly something occurs to me.

"Wait!" I call out. "You forgot the..."

"Pole?" someone interrupts.

It's Kevin! He's been watching us and is finally scheming to make the situation better, not worse. This might be the first time Kevin's ever helped save the day.

Todd grabs the pole from Kevin without missing a beat. Security guards sprint after Todd but he doesn't notice.

"Stop that cheater!" a man screams. But the woman next to him elbows him in the ribs and cheers Todd on.

Todd makes it to fifty feet away from the Ferris wheel where the panda is still screaming.

"Somebody help me, please!" the panda hollers. "I'm afraid of heights!"

With the grace of an acrobat, Todd launches himself toward the Ferris wheel.

All the cameras turn from the opening ceremony to Todd's courageous leap. He flies through the air toward the panda, who reaches for him. The whole crowd gasps as Todd... misses the panda's hand.

What?!

"You've got this!" I shout.

If there's one thing I'm good at, it's encouragement.

Billy's voice rings out across the stadium as well. "You can do it, Todd!"

Everyone begins to cheer, urging Todd on. It works – as soon as Todd's feet are on the ground, he runs back to the pole to try again. Todd and Billy have something in common: they don't give up, no matter how hard things get.

Todd takes another sprint toward the Ferris wheel and vaults toward the panda again. This time the security guards push the onlookers back to give Todd room. The crowd gasps once more – on this try, Todd jumps higher than I've ever seen anyone jump before.

"That must be some kind of record," someone says from the audience.

Todd reaches the top of the Ferris wheel and lands in the same bucket as the panda. Bullseye! Everyone cheers.

But what now? I can see the panda still shaking in fear.

"Get on my back," Todd yells to the panda. "We're going to jump."

"Jump?!" the panda shouts. "We'll both be killed!"

"I'm a pole vaulter," Todd says. "And pole vaulters don't just know how to jump. They also know how to land."

Todd turns and calls to the crowd: "Quick! Bring over the landing pad!"

A group of spectators runs to the side of the arena where the landing pad is set up for tomorrow's pole vaulting competition. They try to lift the pad but it's too heavy. Several other fans run over to help. The group slowly carries the pad across the field, dropping it right below the Ferris wheel.

The panda is still afraid, but there doesn't seem to be another way to get down. He bravely climbs onto Todd's back.

If Todd is afraid, he doesn't show it. "Get ready," he instructs the panda. "I'm going to jump in three... two..."

The whole audience is silent. Everyone's eyes are on Todd.

"ONE!" Todd shouts.

He springs out of the passenger car with the panda on his back. It feels like they're falling in slow motion.

Finally they reach the pad, bouncing several times before landing.

The audience gives Todd a standing ovation. The panda climbs off the pad and pulls Todd into a bear hug.

"Todd is a hero!" someone shouts.

"Invite Todd back!" another voice yells.

A woman begins to chant: "One more chance. One more chance."

The panda dances, to the crowd's delight. When the Ferris wheel finally begins to turn again, everyone applauds.

 "We have important news," says the announcer. "We just

received the results of Todd's tinkle test. Between that and his heroic rescue of Panji, Todd Brown is allowed to compete in this year's Olympic Games!"

Everyone cheers. Considering he saved the Olympics, it only seems fair for Todd to be let back into the competition. I always knew Todd wasn't a cheater, but I'm glad the rest of the world knows now too.

It's one of the happiest moments of my life. Through the crowd I see Billy, whose smile is almost as big as mine.

#GameTime

The next day is the pole vaulting competition. I get there early to get a good spot and find Billy already there with an open seat next to him.

"I saved it for you," he says. "I wanted to be sure the *other* person who saved the Olympics got a good seat."

"It was the least I could do," I say.

"Where's Dot?" Billy asks.

"She decided to go to the soccer game. Unfortunately, it's at the same time as this," I admit.

Billy laughs. "She deserves to see her favorite sport."

There are only two minutes until the competition begins; everyone takes out their phone to record the event.

Billy and I watch the pole vaulting together, cheering politely for everyone who isn't Todd. It's a close competition: two athletes have jumped eighteen feet, one jumped eighteen and a half, and one jumped nearly nineteen feet.

Finally, it's the moment we've been waiting for.

 "Please welcome TODD BROWN!" the announcer calls.

The crowd goes wild. Billy and I leap to our feet, cheering loudest of all. Only he and I know how much had to happen in order to make this moment possible.

Todd enters the arena and waves to his fans. He's clearly the audience favorite.

Someone else joins him on the field: Panji, who performs a hip hop dance as Todd warms up.

"That is one grateful panda," Billy says.

With his pole in hand, Todd takes a running start and makes a flying leap.

"Eighteen feet, four inches!" the announcer shouts. "Third place! That gives hometown favorite Todd Brown the Bronze."

Everyone cheers, but Billy is disappointed. "He should've come in first after what he did last night."

"But Billy," I say. "Third place in the Olympics is great! And besides, you don't need to come in first to be a hero."

Kevin walks by with a giant bucket of popcorn; his robot SAM follows closely behind.

"At least Todd didn't come in number two," Kevin laughs. "Get it? A number two, getting number two."

Billy and I ignore him.

"You're right," Billy tells me. "My brother, the Bronze medalist!"

"Todd's a hero!" I shout.

To my surprise, the whole crowd chants back. "TODD'S A HERO!"

I suddenly understand how Billy felt a few weeks ago when Todd was first selected for the Olympic team because right now I feel like a hero too.

After celebrating with Todd, Billy and I meet up with Dot in between soccer games. We watch a few games together then run off to hang with our parents, texting each other for the rest of the afternoon.

It's a great day to be an emoji.

#LeaveUsAReview

Please support us by leaving a review.
The more reviews we get, the more
books we will write.

#FollowUsOnInstagram
@AnnieEmoji * @KevinEmoji

#TeamAnnie

#TeamKevin

#BooksInTheSeries

Horse Party * Emoji Olympics
Call of Doodie * Reality TV

#MakeaCameo

Want to be a Character in the next Emoji

Adventures Book? Enter at:

www.EmojiAdventuresBook.com

www.MontagePublishing.com

MONTAGE PUBLISHING

CPSIA information can be obtained
at www.ICGtesting.com
Printed in the USA
LVOW04s1554190416

484332LV00018B/708/P